I0631757

Interactive Press
Tchaikovsky (Almost) in Love

Dr David Reiter is an award-winning text and digital artist, and Publisher / CEO at IP (Interactive Publications Pty Ltd). Twice winner of the QLD Premier's Award, recent works include the digital narratives *Time Lords Remixed: a Dr Who Poetical* (2020); *Black Books Publishing* (2018), a satire about the publishing industry; the medical/micro-textual hybrid *Timelord Dreaming*, which won the 2016 Western Australian Premier's Award for Digital Narrative, *Your eBook Survival Kit*, now in its 4th edition, and the picture book *Bringing Down the Wall*, which was 2014 Best Book for Teens & Kids (Canadian Children's Book Centre). As artist-in-residence twice at the Banff Centre for the Arts (Canada), he completed *My Planets Reunion Memoir Project*, which won the 2012 WA Premier's Award, and *The Gallery* (2000), a non-linear interactive work about the relationship between Paul Gauguin and Vincent van Gogh, which became a radio play, *Paul & Vincent*, twice broadcast on ABC Radio National's *Poetica*, and a live production in Brisbane. His first script, *Piano in the Garden*, had a rehearsed reading with the QTC under David Berthold. IP recently published his *Outer Space, Inner Minds* (2021) which featured creatives and scientists from ANZ and North America. His work-in-progress is a hybrid work about being Jewish, *Stranger in a Familiar Land*.

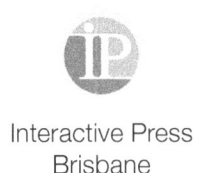

Interactive Press
Brisbane

Interactive Press
an imprint of IP (Interactive Publications Pty Ltd)
Treetop Studio • 9 Kuhler Court
Carindale, Queensland, Australia 4152
sales@ipoz.biz
http://ipoz.biz/shop
First published by IP in 2024
© 2024 David P. Reiter (text); IP (design)

Printed in 12 pt Times New Roman

ISBN: 9781922830890 (PB) 9781922830906

Other scripts and digital media by David P Reiter:
Paul & Vincent
Hemingway in Spain
My Planets Reunion Memoir
Black Books Publishing
Timelord Dreaming
Time Lords Remixed

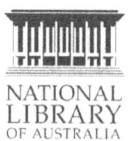

A catalogue record for this book is available from the National Library of Australia

Tchaikovsky (Almost) In Love

A Three-Act Play in Verse

David P. Reiter

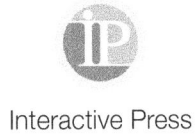

Interactive Press

The Back Story

PYOTR ILICH Tchaikovsky and NADEZHDA von Meck had an impossible relationship. They shared a passion for music and the emotions it could evoke, transcending the complexities of everyday life.

Nadezhda had an unquenchable admiration for Tchaikovsky's music and supported him, as well as several of his contemporaries, mostly notably Nikolai Rubinstein and Claude Debussy, but it was with Tchaikovsky that the boundary between platonic and erotic love became blurred for her.

Though Tchaikovsky may have hinted, in his letters to her, that he preferred men to women for physical love, it's not clear that she got the message. Or, if she did, that she accepted what this would mean for their relationship. Indeed, she seemed to realise that distance would have to be maintained between them, given his inability or reluctance to divorce his wife, and even when Tchaikovsky took up residence at one of her properties after his departure from the Moscow Conservatorium.

For his part, Tchaikovsky went beyond the bounds of gratitude in dedicating works such as his *Symphony No. 4* to her. But it is in his opera Eugene Onegin that he seems to grapple with his conflicting emotions toward Nadezhda to the point at the opera's end that she ultimately rejects him.

This verse play is largely based on my research into the extensive correspondence[3]—some 1200 letters over 14 years—between Tchaikovsky and Nadezhda and does at

times 'read between the lines' to dramatise what I interpreted
as a subtext beneath the words expressed by the characters.
The play's climax comes when the two chance into each
other while on a walk in the forest on the von Meck estate
at Simaki. Most historians maintain that they never actually
met supposedly not to give oxygen to gossips, but the
subtext of the letters suggests a secret yearning, especially
on Nadezhda's part. The play therefore underscores what
might have been in different circumstances and in a more
contemporary setting where a person's passions escape the
bounds of artistic expression.

The Characters

PYOTR ILICH Tchaikovsky (1840-1893). The composer met Nadezhda von Meck in his mid-thirties, around the time of his marriage to Antonina Miliukova in 1877.

Nine years his senior, NADEZHDA von Meck (1831-1894) was a bit sensitive about their age difference but forged ahead with their 'relationship' only a year after her husband's Karl's death, leaving her in a wealthy position.

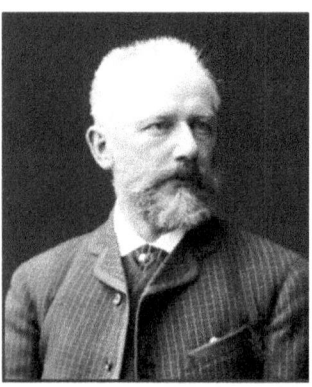 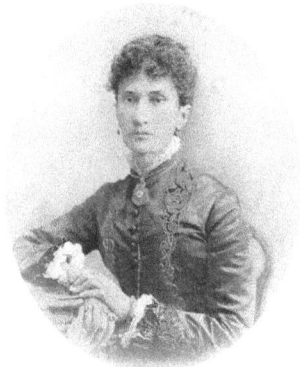

The Setting

The Theatre: preferably a conventional space, with the audience facing the stage. Theatre-in-the-round is possible, but with the SCREENS occupying a quarter of audience seating.

The Screens: Three separate wide-angle screens will be used, although a single wide screen or monitor could be substituted, allowing for three areas of simultaneous or sequential projection. All the A/V sources are available online via the links provided in the Sources section.

Audio: Surround sound, if possible, for the projected contents (opera, symphony, etc)

Stage props: Minimalist period pieces. Key furniture: two wooden writing DESKS and period CHAIRS. A PODIUM. An array of MUSIC STANDS and orchestral CHAIRS, with a few INSTRUMENTS, including a VIOLIN, CELLO and PIANO, preferably a GRAND. Optional: a few cardboard cut-outs of PLAYERS to be leant against the CHAIRS.

A Note on Multimedia:

The STAGE DIRECTIONS may seem prescriptive about the multimedia elements to be included, but they are intended to be suggestive and inspirational.

For example, I have provided precise timeframes for the A/V elements, but these can be extended, shortened, or even completely changed, depending on the producer's wishes and the overall timing of the play.

It may be more practical to record and archive the multimedia elements for use offline rather than relying on internet connectivity.

The written play provides links acknowledging online sources. For copyright reasons, these acknowledgements should be included with programs provided at the performance.

ACT 1

SCENE 1: THEY MEET IN MUSIC

SETTING: A minimalist stage, except for some music stands and chairs with various instruments, especially a CELLO and VIOLIN, scattered about, a PODIUM at STAGE FRONT CENTRE and two period chairs with WRITING DESKs and drawers, STAGE LEFT and STAGE RIGHT, slightly face each other. On PYOTR ILICH's desk there is a carafe of wine and a goblet half-full of RED WINE. There should be sufficient room STAGE FRONT for the characters to wander among the orchestra chairs and address the audience, and pockets of space for the characters to retreat to as required. At stage rear are THREE LARGE SCREENS for projections. One is STAGE CENTRE; the others are at STAGE LEFT and STAGE RIGHT, respectively.

AT RISE: As the audience comes in, the FIRST MOVEMENT OF PYOTR ILICH TCHAIKOVSKY'S *SYMPHONY NO. 4* (0.08-2.35)[1] is playing CENTRE SCREEN as background music, with visuals being projected on the RIGHT and LEFT SCREENS. Gradually the MUSIC fades out, along with the lighting. PYOTR ILICH, and NADEZHDA, wearing a DINNER PARTY GOWN, enter STAGE LEFT and RIGHT, respectively and begin to speak with VISUALS from the music playing on their faces. They utter the same phrase, over and over, but with different nuances varying from controlled formality to intimate intensity, apprehensive to excited, celebratory to mournful. The pacing of their dialogue at first is slow, with each character speaking softly in turn, then gradually accelerating to the point where their speech overlaps and they are shouting over each other's head.

---

[1] https://www.youtube.com/watch?v=VMTBLuMzvs0&t=2315s

PYOTR ILICH

Dearest…friend,
Dearest…friend,
Dearest…friend, etc…

NADEZHDA

Dearest…friend,
Dearest…friend,
Dearest…friend, etc…

*(There's a moment of silence where all we can
hear is their breathlessness. Then the LIGHTING
comes up, dissecting the stage with colour, e.g.,
green for PYOTR ILICH's sector, as he speaks,
gold for NADEZHDA's, as she speaks. PYOTR
ILICH's holding an ENVELOPE, staring at it with
mixed emotions. NADEZHDA, writing a LETTER
on her DESK, seems to respond to the emotions he
displays. Finally, he walks to the PODIUM, and,
bathed in a BLUE SPOTLIGHT and facing the audience, tears open the envelope and begins to read
it, silently mouthing the words as NADEZHDA
writes/speaks. His mood changes from one of an-
ticipation to horror. THE LIGHTING steadily dims
on him until he is in semi-darkness. Both address
the audience rather than each other.)*

NADEZHDA

Dearest Peter Il'ich,
I hardly know how to begin.
It is taking every ounce
of my strength to set pen
to paper.

My financial affairs have complicated
to the point where I find myself
on the brink

of ruin.

Still, I have done all in my power
to protect you from loss,
painfully aware
as I am of the promises
I have made you.

Let me assure you that
what I am about to say
in no way deflates
the very high
regard I have for you,
or the weight
I place on the… friendship
I hope still remains
between us.

> ### PYOTR ILICH
> *(returns to the lighting of his sector
> and seizes on her words)*

'*Remains*'?
Is there not *immortal* life
in what shelters
in our memories?

> ### NADEZHDA
> *(ruffled, as though anticipating his
> reaction)*

You can take comfort for now
from the surplus of applause
that greets your every performance.

> ### PYOTR ILICH
> *(correcting her)*

Now.

If only that lasted as long

as a life—or beyond it,
NADEZHDA Filaretovna!

NADEZHDA

You will be fine without me.
You were almost fine with me
before our words tricked us.
Don't you see? Our mindful
contact will only undercut
your expected good fortune.

PYOTR ILICH

Let them gossip
all they like!!

They are but aberrant notes –
misled by yesterday's broadsheet
then discarded for damp fish-wrap

NADEZHDA
*(rises from her desk, trembling,
holding a LETTER at arm's
length)*
My inkwell patience runs dry,
so I've ended your allowance
and promise not write to you again.

If our friendship over the past
thirteen years means anything to you,
please do not try to change my mind.

I must be in deadly earnest,
which is for the best
for your music
(whispers)
and for me…

So farewell, my dearest, irreplaceable

friend. Do not forget the heart
whose… sympathy for you is… boundless!
> *(still clutching her PEN, she drops the
> LETTER, sinks down to the right of the
> PODIUM, fighting back tears)*

PYOTR ILICH

NO!!!
I will not allow that.
> *(tears up her LETTER, tosses it into
> the air in front of him, watches the
> pieces drifting down)*

SCENE 2: THE PAST IS NEVER PAST

SETTING: *Same minimalist stage.*

AT RISE: *BLACKOUT. NADEZHDA exits. A few measures from the final scene of DON GIOVANNI (1.30.56-1.31.37) FADE IN, with VISUALS on the CENTRE SCREEN. As the lights come up, PYOTR ILICH wanders disconsolately to the chair with a cello, STAGE CENTRE, readies the bow and plays a single discordant chord, visualised on the LEFT and RIGHT SCREENS. DON GIOVANNI fades out.*

PYOTR ILICH

She hated Mozart.
Can you believe it?
Mozart? Don Giovanni is the best
opera ever written. Yes, yes,
perhaps Wolfy spread his art too thinly,
even for his brief interlude on Earth
but I love his music so much
that I won't admit his critics.

He composed as the nightingale sings
at dusk. It is to him
that I dedicate
the remains of my stay on Earth
to music.
> *(senses NADEZHDA, in a black gown, entering STAGE RIGHT, behind him)*

I never doubted NADEZHDA Filaretovna, either.
Except for her dislike of him.

NADEZHDA

I grant that his music was… daring,
for its time.
But I much prefer your depth, power, grandeur.

PYOTR ILICH

(gasps)
I swear, if you hadn't been so
well… endowed—

NADEZHDA

(comes up behind him and hesitantly
wraps her arms around him)
Ah, and so the truth
comes out! You *did* think me
a beauty—back then!

(startled, he turns in her direction, but
she ducks the other way)

PYOTR ILICH

I didn't mean—

NADEZHDA

How can you be so godly
certain of what you meant
or didn't mean?

PYOTR ILICH

Because I wrote it all down.

In strict notation.

NADEZHDA

Liar! No one writes everything down!

Some notes must be left
to enjoy their silence.

> *(She drifts to the middle of her sector*
> *of the stage as he does to his. They*
> *speak in each other's general direction*
> *but avoid each other's eyes.)*

PYOTR ILICH

So why did you forsake me?

NADEZHDA

I didn't.
I just stopped writing.

PYOTR ILICH

You must know you were the only
woman who ever mattered to me!

NADEZHDA

But not the only one. Just recall
when we started.
> *(sits, arms and legs crossed)*

PYOTR ILICH

> *(remembering, and steps in front*
> *as KOTEK's PHOTO[2] appears on*
> *the CENTRE SCREEN, blows him*
> *a cautious kiss, then turns to the*
> *audience)*

It was Iosif Kotek, my dear pupil,
who first told me
Nadezhda was interested in me.
> *(moves to the chair with a VIOLIN,*
> *sits, plays a note that anticipates the*
> *clip from his VIOLIN CONCERTO*
> *in D MAJOR played by RAY CHEN*
> *(01.56-02.25)[3], projected on the*

---

[2] https://bit.ly/3zejQSM
[3] https://www.youtube.com/watch?v=VMov701K_7A

*LEFT SCREEN. The music fades
as NADEZHDA continues, with the
PHOTO of KOTEK with PYOTR
ILICH dissolving from the CENTRE
SCREEN.)*

NADEZHDA

I only mentioned your music, dearest friend.
I would not have shared anything more
with such a man.

PYOTR ILICH

(to her)
You wronged him.

NADEZHDA

So you said.

PYOTR ILICH

He was only young.

Did he tell you
about my health problems?

NADEZHDA

I felt your depression
as if it were my own.
                    *(CUE IN: THE TEMPEST (02.32-
                    03.14)[4], after which she adds)*
But then I heard your *Tempest*,
which left me dizzy
with daydreams.

PYOTR ILICH

Is that why you offered me so much money
with hardly any strings?

NADEZHDA

---

[4] https://www.youtube.com/watch?v=fEKVsNoQMCY

There are always strings
with money—however invisible.

PYOTR ILICH

Why me?
Why just then?

NADEZHDA

I was at interval.
My Karl had died,
and he had left me too much money.

Somehow, *you* made perfect sense.

PYOTR ILICH

How did he die?
You never said.

NADEZHDA

Heart attack.
Out of the blue.

PYOTR ILICH

He must have been young!

NADEZHDA

Not so young. But Fate
was unkind to him.

PYOTR ILICH

Did you... love him?

NADEZHDA

I parented eleven children with him!

Eighteen, if you count
those that God saw fit
to let fly in innocence.

PYOTR ILICH

Children are always the evidence,
seldom the verdict.

But did you love him?

NADEZHDA

Such a word is not sufficient
to sum up a relationship.

He was a petty engineer who expected
nothing more from the future
than a paycheque.
Until I nagged him to resign.

We were down to our last twenty kopecks
before I steered him to the railway
where he made our fortune
in a small curtesy to chance
and a bow to my business sense.

PYOTR ILICH

Not much of a pillar, then?

NADEZHDA

Life did him no favours.
And there wasn't a speck
of music in him!

PYOTR ILICH
*(onto the PODIUM, extending his
hands to the audience)*
Some of us are meant to compose,
others to merely listen… and appreciate.

NADEZHDA
(circles her DESK)

There's an art to audience

if you listen with your soul.

Do you remember what I said after
you sent me your first compositions?

PYOTR ILICH

No.
> *(he returns to his DESK, extracts a*
> *LETTER from a DRAWER)*

But here it is.
> *(he begins reading, with her miming as*
> *she writes at her DESK)*

NADEZHDA / PYOTR ILICH

Being admired by a person so musically
insignificant as myself...

NADEZHDA

> *(finishing)*

might seem ridiculous to you,
but please believe that your music
does make life fresher for me.

Call me a crank,
but do not laugh at me.

PYOTR ILICH

It was such a strange
letter that I had to write back
immediately.
> *(returns to his DESK, scribbles)*

NADEZHDA

> *(laughing, sits at her DESK)*

You thanked me for offering so much money
for so little music!

PYOTR ILICH

I couldn't help myself.
I already felt a sympathy for you
owing to your sympathy for me.

NADEZHDA

You said, 'I know you better
than you perhaps think.'

Did you think I was hiding something?

PYOTR ILICH
*(a <u>PHOTO of PYOTR ILICH</u>[5] appears
on the MIDDLE SCREEN, slowly
zooming in, as he reads from the
LETTER)*

Yes, and it was always about me
back then. You asked for my photograph.

Here it is again.

NADEZHDA

I have two already, but I want one from you.
It will help me to replay those feelings
in your music that send me spinning
with the desires that life cannot foster.

PYOTR ILICH
*(rises from his chair and addresses the
audience, laughing)*

In short, a hopeless romantic.

NADEZHDA
(still writing)

My ideal companion is a… musician,
but with a personality equal
to his talent.

---

[5] https://www.musicwithease.com/tchaikovsky-pictures.html

If there is less of a man
in him, his music will seem no more
than a deception to exploit
innocent listeners.

PYOTR ILICH
(turns to wink at the audience)
We have all been entertained
by cads like that!
(back in her direction)
Then you asked me to write you
a funeral march.
How odd!

NADEZHDA
A piano duet, Pyotr Ilich, if you please.
One that I can practice
even master—to my skills.

Give me the chance
to echo life for a moment,
even as mine draws to a close.

PYOTR ILICH
Were you really intent on cheating death?

I sent you a faded photograph, asking…
*(closes his eyes as he recites, and she
echoes)*

PYOTR ILICH / NADEZHDA
Why do you need this as well,
if it's my music that you love?

PYOTR ILICH
(to the audience)
I hoped that would keep

her on the game. But…

NADEZHDA
(writing)
Dearest friend, your spectre
lights up my world
teasing away the darkness.

If I had this much
sunlight in wealth
I would banish it all
to you.

PYOTR ILICH

Pure gush!

Yet there was something about her
that I couldn't corner
with words.

NADEZHDA

Your music makes me forget all
those hurtful things.

My nerves tingle.
I want to sob with joy,
I want to soar above the earth,
my temples throbbing,
my eyes misting over
from the rare air.

PYOTR ILICH
(laughs)
That's what comes of a bad day's work
and too many glasses of cheap wine.

But then she tried to soften me up
with her photograph.

NADEZHDA
(pulls a PHOTO from the DRAWER
and holds it up)
This is me with my youngest, Milochka.
(writes)
She asks to whom I am writing,
and when I say it is to someone
special she mistakes you for a king:
"*Et pourquoi est-ce que tu n'écris*
pas au Roi de la Bavière?"

PYOTR ILICH
Have I ever even been
to Bavaria?
(toasts with the empty GOBLET)
Of course—Vienna!

Sweet Milochka—
every bit her mother's child.

One of eighteen lives
composed by her and engineer Karl.

NADEZHDA
(quickly)
I finished with 'I entrust all
my feelings and wishes to you,
and I'm sure I am not making a mistake
this time.'

PYOTR ILICH
(clutches himself, stifling a laugh)
First the daughter imagines me
as the King of Bavaria,
then the mother sees me
as the chess piece mate to her mistakes!

NADEZHDA
(to the audience)
Well, why write music at all, if not
to make people fall in love with you
between the notes?

PYOTR ILICH
I might have ended it right there.

I could have cobbled together a pale
ditty and demanded much more
than it was worth.

That would have stilled the wind
from her sails!

NADEZHDA
But you didn't.
And we know why!

PYOTR ILICH
(preciously)
Sometimes stray notes corner their harmony
despite the composer's better judgement.
(to the audience)
Besides, she was so rich!

NADEZHDA
I *did* ask you to address me as "thou".

It was the least
you could have done.

PYOTR ILICH
(shudders)
Yes, it was just as well
that Fate played *that* trump card.
(singing)

A 'Thou' before bed
and soon Ye be wed.

Who hummed that?

> NADEZHDA
> *(to the audience)*
> Certainly not star-crossed Juliet!

(extends her hands to him)

His marriage was more like a sham
joker than a poised trump!

> PYOTR ILICH
> Marriage wasn't my idea.

But it couldn't have come
at a more... starless time.

> NADEZHDA
> He dedicates a symphony to me one minute
> then stumbles off to get hitched the next!
> > *(holds up a LETTER, miming as he
> > reads)*

> PYOTR ILICH
> Dearest friend,
> Back in May, this girl sent a letter
> saying she'd fallen in love with me.
> Hopelessly.

What could I do but write back?

> NADEZHDA
> Lucky girl!

> PYOTR ILICH
> I made it clear that I felt no debt
> for her luck.

NADEZHDA

And that was that?

PYOTR ILICH

No. She wrote back to say
her life would be over
if we did not marry.

Without even a preamble!
And certainly not a climax!

NADEZHDA
(suspicious)
If you promised her nothing,
you must have owed her less!

PYOTR ILICH

I swear I did everything
 to put her off.

I painted myself as irritable,
unsociable, and, above all, poor
then asked her if she still loved me.

Horrors of horrors, she said yes!
She never expected the composer
of her dreams to be rich.
Or so she said.

NADEZHDA

You should have just thanked her
and walked away!

PYOTR ILICH

She was so certain of me
that I sensed a destiny in it:
I must be married.

NADEZHDA

This had nothing to do with your perch
at the Conservatory?

PYOTR ILICH

Ah, ha!

It did quiet some prattling tongues—
but only for a month or so.

NADEZHDA
*(scribbling furiously, her body
language undercutting her words)*
Don't hide your essence under a bushel, my dear.
If you make another person happy,
even by chance,
you will reap some happiness, too.

PYOTR ILICH
(narrows his eyes)
You must swear not to tell anyone of this.
No one knows about my fate but you!
Swear!

NADEZHDA
(to the audience)
I replied it was up to him
to correct his mistake.
But she reeled him in so quickly
after that!

*(NADEZHDA appears on the RIGHT
SCREEN in a WEDDING DRESS,
angrily clutching WILTED FLOWERS)*

PYOTR ILICH

Dearest friend,
All our money has gone
on the wedding, but—

NADEZHDA
(in unison with her double on the screen)
You mean my money?

PYOTR ILICH

Of course.
All I had back then
was by your good graces.

I lived in hope that some fortune
could grow out of the idle soil
of misfortune.

Antonina owned a forest near Klin
worth at least 4,000 roubles,
enough for an apartment in Moscow.

But she's been swindled
and now we have nothing
but debts.

Worst of all, I am completely
unable to work.

(NADEZHDA on the screen fades)

NADEZHDA
(with a secret smile)
When I read your letter, Pyotr Ilich,
my heart overflowed with sorrow.
You seemed so sad and harassed.

So, take this purse and find a cure
in the Caucasus, while your dear wife
sees to furnishing your apartment
with seconds.

I wish you healing in time.
But do remember me
when the curtain
falls!

PYOTR ILICH

You were right again.

I should have reneged, but I was so petrified
by dislike for my wife, and the fear
my musicality would be lost forever.

So, I returned to Moscow where we dragged on
for several murderous days.

I drank at every pause,
which won me scant breaths of oblivion,
so I could spend evenings with my Kotek,
who is closer to me now than a first… son.

The most dazzling thing
is that Antonina really does seem to love me
though I cannot be more than sorry for her.

NADEZHDA

Tears dimmed my eyes when I read that,
and I wondered where is the justice
that pins the most deserving people
with the spears of unforgiving time?

I do not wear rose-tinted glasses,
but now and then we must make
the best of a familiar sorrow
and hope for at least a sepia life.

*(As the LIGHTS FADE, SFX of distant
GUNFIRE)*

ACT 2

SCENE 1: FRAGILE PEACE IN WAR

SETTING: *Same minimalist stage.*

AT RISE: *RED BACKGROUND LIGHTING comes up.*
PYOTR on the STAGE, cross-legged and leaning
on the PODIUM, flinching at the GUNFIRE and
EXPLOSIONS. Some of the CHAIRS and MUSIC
STANDS have toppled. NADEZHDA faces him
from her DESK.

CUE IN: SYMPHONY NO. 4 (0:35 to 1:55),[6] with VISUAL-
ISATION on the LEFT and RIGHT SCREENS,
while MIDDLE SCREEN shows clips from the af-
termath of bombing of civilian targets in Ukraine,
which continue after the music has finished.

PYOTR ILICH
(snaps out of a daze)
Sorry.
I was thinking about the war.
Not *the* war, but wars to come
and their orphans of peace
searching in vain
for a nesting place.

So, how are things for you in Brailov?

NADEZHDA
Thank God you didn't go to the Caucasus.
Many troops march, march, march by here daily,
singing brashly of the glory they think
they've won.

---

[6] https://www.youtube.com/watch?v=VMTBLuMzvs0&t=2315s

I sponsor a hospital for two hundred,
and have invited their officers to dinner,
where they defame Turks they've never met.
       (pauses)
But now one's been killed and another
seriously wounded, disarming their families
to grief. How inhuman war is!

PYOTR ILICH
      (returns to his DESK and snaps up his
      PEN)

Dearest friend,
how should I complain
when our country burbles with streams
of blood? The least I can do
is to be more patient with my wife
and discover those layers in her
I may have missed.
      (nods to the audience)
I did put on a brave front for Nadezhda Filaretovna.

Even as I confronted the pain of our soldiers
the wound in here
      (beats his chest)
was even greater.
Somehow, I distracted myself
by composing.

NADEZHDA

It's been days since you have written,
and I am desperate for some calm. Tell me
how it goes with our symphony.

PYOTR ILICH

Good news!

Some progress… at last.

The first movement will be harder to score
because it is complicated and long, but I think
it will be the best. The three remaining ones
are simple enough and will be great fun
to orchestrate. The Scherzo will introduce
an instrumental effect from which I expect
great things.

NADEZHDA

I am *so* happy to hear this.
I knew that your inertia
could not last for long.

The alternating sections of orchestra you propose
will be original and, no doubt, very beautiful.

My life is always better for your music,
so please do not keep me in suspense.
                    (pauses)
Now that I feel reassured about your health,
I will pack for Lago di Como.

How I dread
the coming of winter here!

PYOTR ILICH

And, just like that, she was gone,
but not before sending my allowance,
plus an afterthought of 3,000 roubles,
by special messenger…

PYOTR ILICH / NADEZHDA

…in case of some… unexpected.

PYOTR ILICH

I almost missed her.

No, I *did* feel her absence!

> NADEZHDA

How excruciatingly good and yet unbearable
life can be! Nature teases us with the sense
that there is such a goal as happiness.

Yet, whenever we reach out to grasp it,
we find that it's only an elusive songbird.

> PYOTR ILICH

She meant the war, but how her words
compounded the growing ache in my heart.

At least she was rich enough to escape
from danger when she needed to.

> NADEZHDA

Remember, Pyotr Ilich,
it takes more than money
to win freedom.
> *(pauses)*
But don't hold back—are you afraid
of distressing me?

> PYOTR ILICH

So, I told her.
After just a fortnight with my wife,
I've realised that nothing will save us.

I've had flights of madness where I hate her
so much I could strangle her vacant words
of love!

> NADEZHDA

I know now I should have not
left him on his own.

> PYOTR ILICH

> *(writing)*

I *was* mad, dearest friend.

I drank a toxic dram or four
and sank into what I hoped
would be my final dream,
but I was to wake, disappointed.

Or was I disappointed
that I woke at all?

NADEZHDA

Oh, my darling!
Do not retreat into yourself
like that!

PYOTR ILICH

Anatoly was by my bed.
He had concocted an excuse with Rubinstein
that I was ill and needed to go abroad.

So, in the dead of night
he comported me to Lake Geneva
and reassured my wife
that she would be called
to follow soon.

But, like our imagined peace,
that will never happen.

NADEZHDA
(scribbling)
You did your best for your *certain personage*,
to the point of sacrificing yourself.

Now you must let those who care about you
take charge until you are fit enough
to tame your mind again.

I hope this finds you ready

to accept the circumstances
you deserve.

PYOTR ILICH

I do not write this to worry you…

NADEZHDA

Dearest, dearest friend.
If only you knew how indispensable
you are to me, and how much I need
you to be true
to yourself!
>   *(sighs)*
Absolutely nothing
that I do is for you.
It's all for me.

By not telling me what is
in your heart, you make me feel so
remote from you, like a chord
in limbo,
and that cuts me deep.

I insist
that you write to me the very instant
you get to Lake Geneva,
and promise not
to hold anything back!

(BLACKOUT)

SCENE 2: WHAT PRICE FREEDOM?

SETTING: *The same minimalist set, except that the CHAIRS are even more in disarray, some half concealing the INSTRUMENTS. A PIANO is positioned BACK STAGE in line with PYOTR ILICH's DESK.*

AT RISE: *Faint and flickering lighting, lingering smoke. SFX: faint EXPLOSIONS and closer GUNFIRE. On the SCREENS FADE IN MIRRORED CLIPS of shelled out apartments, displaced civilians wandering the streets with meagre belongings. FADE TO BLACK. SFX: running STREAM, CHIRPPING BIRDS.*

   CUE IN ONEGIN 1 from 2.35 to fade out at 3.53.[7] SIDE SPOTS on NADEZHDA and PYOTR ILICH as they resume writing at their DESKS. Replenished CARAFE of RED WINE on PYOTR'S DESK

PYOTR ILICH
(writing)
I awoke by the lake today.
It is pleasant enough,
but somewhat dreary with mist.

The mountains frighten me.
The sun is shadowed by clouds,
and the hurried rain
consigns the scene to a stormy
grey._____

[7] https://www.youtube.com/watch?v=l_pYA5N4T4k

Thank God you are sending me the means
to go to Italy!

My sister has moved my wife
to her place in the country
away from the gossips,
and I pray that I need not
set eyes on that *certain personage*
again.

Only from retrospect do I see
her true nature. Her head and heart
are lonely, and she has never spurted
a single idea.

She showed no interest in my work
until the day before I left
when she asked if my piano pieces
could be bought at Jurgenson's.

Imagine!

NADEZHDA
Here is your money for Italy,
and some extra for good luck.
If what you say is true of your wife—
and I am sure it is—
she will not sob for long.

> *(a thin GOLD SPOTLIGHT shines
> from above to one side of him)*

PYOTR ILICH
Sunshine at last!

I sought your Dr Saligoux in Milan,
but to no avail. I ended up at the mercy
of a certain Dr Archambault,

who said that my malady is incurable,
but it need not prevent me from living
to a hundred.

His script comprised four demands:
1. chew a special breed of chalk
before breakfast and dinner,
2. drain a glass of *Hauterive* water
a quarter of an hour before food,
3. take the cure at the *bains de Barèges*
and 4) avoid a huge range of foodstuffs.

And he expected to be paid handsomely
for this insult!

Thank you so much for the annuity of 6,000.
It is, as usual, far too much, but I promise
I shall dedicate every piece of music to you
that I write from now on.

I have thought a great deal
about you these past days.
And I… love you dearly.

NADEZHDA
(bathed in RED LIGHT, from her neck
up)

If saying so brings back
colour to your cheeks, dearest friend,
it is money well-spent.

PYOTR ILICH

How I wish it were so!

Italy is so warm and historical,
but the more cheerful the place is,
the worse it seems for me.

NADEZHDA

Then I urge you to move on to Naples,
where I will have you in touch with
a famous Viennese doctor whose specialty
is puzzle pieces of the mind.

Above all, be cautious with the water, Pyotr Ilich.
Drink mostly seltzer, and just a modest amount
of wine—if you must—
at lunch and dinner.
        (pauses)
So, your wife did not press you for children?
I must say that I have no sympathy at all
with such selfish beings.

Having children so
invests us with the poetry
of life!

PYOTR ILICH

No, for once, you wrong her. It is I
who did not want offspring from her
lest it solidify her claim on me
until they could be banished.

        *(SCREEN RIGHT shows IMAGE of ST
        MARK'S SQUARE)*[8]

Do you know what maddens me in Venice?
In St Mark's Square, all you hear from the mob
hiding from the sun in the shadow

        *(SCREEN LEFT shows IMAGE of ST
        MARK'S BELL TOWER)*[9]

---

[8] https://acrobat.adobe.com/id/urn:aaid:sc:AP:0a54e965-7102-4c6c-8ca5-d01183b895d6
[9] https://acrobat.adobe.com/id/urn:aaid:sc:AP:fee9ccb6-29f6-4759-b43c-f4ca5fb29677

of the Bell Tower with their goblets
of wine is '*Vittoria di Turchi!*'

Why don't they shout about the real
Russian victories rather than the invented
Turkish ones?

God! When will this terrible war end?

No room for saving face—
it seems one side or the other
must be crushed!

                    NADEZHDA
Do not dwell on things
you cannot revise, my darling.
Help us survivors escape
on the wings of your music!

                    PYOTR ILICH
You are right to recast my energies.
I think you are so in sympathy
with my music because we both yearn
for the same elusive ideal.

I really would have gone quite loony
without my music.

It is heaven's gift
to us as we clamour after light
concealed by the darkness.

                    NADEZHDA
Is Italy really so bad for you?

                    PYOTR ILICH
         (laughs)
The further away from Russia I move,
the more Russian I become.

*(IMAGE of ROZHDESTVENSKY
BOULEVARD[10] in winter fades in and
out on the MIDDLE SCREEN. SFX:
HORSE HOOVES and CARRIGES.)*

NADEZHDA

Then you must return, but to a haven
of peace rather than pain.
Won't you call my house
on Rozhdestvensky Boulevard home?

PYOTR ILICH

(nervous)
In a different life, perhaps.
But, in this one… it must be impossible.

NADEZHDA

With me, of course.
But there is so much space,
and all we would share in my absence
would be the staff and our friendship –
in the same way as now.

PYOTR ILICH

I would be happy to live anywhere
that offered complete seclusion.
But would it be so?

*(CUE IN: RIDE OF THE VALKYRIES
(0:00-01.26),[11] projected on all
SCREENS. FADE OUT vision and
audio from 01.10 with last line 'for the
music'.)*

---

[10] https://acrobat.adobe.com/id/urn:aaid:sc:AP:fee9ccb6-29f6-4759-b43c-f4ca5fb29677

[11] https://www.youtube.com/watch?v=s2RiOhYpRFc&list=RDsvMHBPed9Bs&index=4

I've just seen *Die Walküre* here in Vienna.
What a Don Quixote that Wagner is! A genius,
no doubt, but so saturated by theory
he's completely lost sight of the reason
for the music.

I was to leave for Venice tomorrow,
but Kotek is unwell,
and I can't leave him
on his own.
    (pauses)
I would still like to sway your opinion
about this good-natured, kindly boy,
but I'm afraid that I might embarrass
you by mentioning a topic
you might find distasteful.

NADEZHDA

    (hastily)
I know I'm not a distiller of dreams,
but I do believe in the divine spark
of creativity.

If, even the most heartless robber, at the second
he brandishes his knife over a victim,
could hear your music, he would drop his knife
and weep.

PYOTR ILICH

    (pours himself a GLASS OF WINE and
    toasts the audience)
To Venice, then!
With, or without, Richard.
    (takes a gulp)
You were wrong to equate music with intoxication.
Wine will always
have its place. Many use it
to argue that they are well and happy.

(takes another gulp and smiles),
They may pay a high price
for this deception.
But music, my dear,
music itself is not
deception but revelation.

It brings light and joy to mind,
not just for a moment
but forever!

NADEZHDA

You will be sending me our
symphony soon?
I can hardly wait!

PYOTR ILICH

When at last you hear it,
you will know
I was thinking of you
at every bar.
(pauses)
In Moscow, when I thought
all was over for me,
I wrote a note on the draft:
'In the event of my death,
this notebook must
be given to N. F. NADEZHDA.'

Only you could I trust to preserve
the essence of my last composition.

NADEZHDA
(to the audience)
Who could not love him for that?
(scribbles)
Russia so misses you, Pyotr Ilich.

(As she continues, IMAGES of the named composers ([12] *,* [13] *,* [14] *,* [15] *) are projected on SCREENS, LEFT to RIGHT, FADE OUT on cue to clips of RUBINSTEIN,* [16] *PROJECTED on all three SCREENS)*

We have only that lifeless Rimsky-Korsakov,
witless Borodin, misguided Cui
and that has-been Mussorgsky.

I could be fond of Rubinstein,
but I… adore *you*, my friend.

Just say the word,
and I'll send you
a first-class fare!

PYOTR ILICH
As it happens, I'm thinking of Russia
at this very moment. A summer walk
through the country meadows,
over the steppes,
exerting to the point
of exhaustion,
hearing the music
of a whispering rivulet,
in the distance a simple
little church… bliss!
(pauses)
So, I went to the post office this morning,

[12] https://en.wikipedia.org/wiki/Nikolai_Rimsky-Korsakov#/media/File:Rimsky-Korsakov_Serow_crop.png

[13] https://bit.ly/3B2nIH9

[14] https://en.wikipedia.org/wiki/César_Cui#/media/File:Cesar_Cui_by_Makovsky_(cropped).jpg

[15] https://www.dallassymphony.org/community-education/dso-kids/listen-watch/composers/modest-mussorgsky/

[16] https://www.youtube.com/watch?v=RbixcDZQIuQ

hoping for a letter from you. Instead,
there was this letter offering to appoint me
delegate to the music section
of the Paris Exhibition.

> *(MIDDLE SCREEN projects*
> *DRAWING of PARIS EXPOSITION;*[17]
> *FADE OUT on 'dark cranny')*

I need your advice now!
How can I represent my country
when I'm still so unwell?
Would I survive eight months
of such slavery?

If you and Modeste told me to go, I would,
and damn the consequences,
but I'd rather starve by degree
in some dark cranny.

NADEZHDA

You were right to refuse Paris, my love.
Otherwise, you would not finish *Onegin*
for the performance before the Grand Duke,
who is, by all accounts,
very impressed with you.

The news from the war front
is good, but Turkey has no money
for reparations, and I'm assured
we will not be offered Bulgaria.

So, I spent all day immersed
in your *First Quartet*,
which cooled so well
my desperate melancholy.

---

[17] https://www.abc.net.au/listen/classic/read-and-watch/music-reads/classically-curious-debussy-paris/11174540

I want to weep
until my heart revives.

Won't you come home?

PYOTR ILICH
I'd be happy to have *Onegin* tried first
at the Conservatory.
> *(CUE IN: TCHAIKOVSKY'S 'CORAL'*
> *ROMANCE (04.44-06.30);*[18] *FADE*
> *OUT on 'like Orlov')*
The students there may be slight,
but they'll be better than prima donna
potbellies like Dodonov
or scoundrels like Orlov.

Rubinstein and Samarin
will save my face
with the Grand Duke.
Of course, I don't expect
the opera will ever make it
to a big stage,
especially in Petersburg.

NADEZHDA
You seem so well now!

I can see you as clearly
as if you were standing right
beside me.

You're smiling through your words.
What a pity I have never actually heard
your voice. Perhaps I can hear it one day
somewhere you could not see me.

---

[18] https://www.youtube.com/watch?v=x_KN4fvavLI

PYOTR ILICH
(scribbling)

I am so enraged by the terms of the truce!
Russia gets nothing but an indemnity
of $500 million,
which Turkey will never pay.

So much spilling of blood,
with so little
edible harvest.

I blame England.
That despicable market-woman
is our real enemy!

(pauses)

This morning, I finished the vocals
for *Onegin*.
But will anyone listen?

NADEZHDA

Pyotr Ilich, have you ever loved?
I think not. You adore music too much
to fall in love with a mortal woman.

I know you once had a platonic
relationship, but that is only
a love tricked by imagination,
not one borne of the heart.
Not something that penetrates
deep into a person's flesh and blood,
without which they cannot survive.

PYOTR ILICH
(to the audience)

There was no sidestepping that one.

(scribbles)
Dearest friend,
if you're asking if I've ever
experienced full happiness in love,
then the answer is no, no
and no again! But if your question is
do I *appreciate* the power
of that emotion, then I can say yes, yes,
and yes again. I want my music to capture
the torments and bliss of love.
You will see that in Olga and Lensky

And, of course, Tatyana and Onegin.
(pauses)
I am puzzled that none
of my Moscow friends have yet reacted
to our symphony. Rubinstein wrote,
in his usual curt fashion,
that it was 'excellently played',
but he said nothing
about the merit of the opera.

NADEZHDA
Pay no attention to him, my love.
The audience received it very well,
especially the Scherzo,
and there was applause a'plenty.

When they called for you,
they had to settle for Rubinstein,
and in fact the orchestra played worse
than I have ever heard it perform.
(pauses)
I have nothing against spiritual love,
as consolation for the real thing,

but it must be with a sincere being.
Otherwise, we're left with only a husk.

PYOTR ILICH

Ah, so it was a success.

I am so glad that you liked it.
> *(wanders over to the UPTURNED*
> *CHAIR concealing the VIOLIN and*
> *rightens them)*

You asked how I compose
when I have no measure
of my subject at the start.
Well, it's a purely invisible
thing. Think of a poet pouring out
verses that demand to be heard,
then add the thousand or more
nuances that the musician has at whim
for inflaming his swirl of notes beyond
the spoken word.

Spiralling with inspiration,
you are transported into mid-air,
and must give voice to your sketch
as each note pummels another
for first attention.
> *(sighs)*

It is so intense that,
if it were to last for more
than a day at a time,
the strings would snap
and the instrument of your mind
would splinter
to extinction.

NADEZHDA

Yes, *yes*. But tell me how
this works for our symphony!

> *(CUE IN SYMPHONY NO. 4, playing*
> *from 0.00[19] then a slow FADE OUT to*
> *0.45 as PYOTR ILICH speaks)*

PYOTR ILICH

I wanted to show how life flits between flaring
dreams and bursts of happiness. There is no escape:
you simply test the sea until you are swamped
and plunged under!

All in a single movement.

NADEZHDA
(sinks to her knees)
You affect my heart with a despair
that exhilarates
yet terrifies.

What a daring sequence
of chords!

> *(CUE IN TRACK 2, SYMPHONY*
> *NO. 4, SECOND MOVEMENT, with*
> *VISUALS from 4.00 to FADE OUT at*
> *5.30.[20] PYOTR ILICH begins speaking*
> *a few measures in, with music FADING*
> *OUT before NADEZHDA speaks.)*

PYOTR ILICH

I know your depression.

You tire from work

---

[19] https://bit.ly/3B2nMqn

[20] https://www.youtube.com/watch?v=e2jGOwWYX6o

and lose yourself in a book
but it slips from your hand
as memories
of youth wash over you.

It is a bitter-sweet past.

NADEZHDA

(rises, unsteadily)
So pensive, yet familiar!

If only I could embrace it.

> *(CUE IN: SYMPHONY NO. 4,*
> *from 30.43.[21] PYOTR ILICH begins*
> *speaking a few measures in, with*
> *music BACKGROUNDING to 31.26*
> *until NADEZHDA speaks.)*

PYOTR ILICH

My Third is made up of capricious
arabesques, images that flash past
your imagination
when you've had just enough
wine to drink.

You see strange pictures,
carousing peasants,
hear a street song.
Somewhere in the distance,
soldiers are marching by.
But these fragments
have nothing to do with daylight:
they are meant
to be wild, incoherent.

---

[21] https://www.youtube.com/watch?v=VMTBLuMzvs0

NADEZHDA

It was so…
original.

And the motif and orchestra were at one.

> *(CUE IN: SYMPHONY NO. 4, from*
> *35.16 to FADE TO BACKGROUND at*
> *36.02.[22] PYOTR ILICH begins speaking*
> *a few measures in, with music FADING*
> *OUT before NADEZHDA speaks.)*

PYOTR ILICH

Finally, some answers.
If you can't find joy in your heart,
connect with the common people.

See how they abandon the worries of the world
to feeling. These are simple but potent
pleasures. Just enough to give you reason
to struggle on.

NADEZHDA

Your Russian strains—how splendid.

How I wish it were possible, Pyotr Ilich,
to thank you in the flesh
for these special words!

PYOTR ILICH
(leans back, gazing up)
How distant we are
from each other!
You in snow,
me framed by a midnight
window.

---

[22] https://www.youtube.com/watch?v=VMTBLuMzvs0

And yet I remember that stubborn
frost giving way to the sudden thaws
of spring.
      (stiffens)
Yet there'll be no warmth or magic
for me until a certain personage
grants me a divorce.

                NADEZHDA

You've asked her
yet again?

                PYOTR ILICH
      (wrings his hands)
Perhaps I can tempt her with a lump sum
rather than that monthly allowance,
which she knows could end too soon
given my precarious state of health.

                NADEZHDA

You are right to lock in
her signature before
you pay her out.
Otherwise, you might never
be free of her.
I'll send what she asks and more
lest she change her mind!

Please don't hesitate
to rely on me, dear friend.
We are at one in your music,
and no one can compete with me
in that.

                PYOTR ILICH
And find me ever deeper

in your debt?
How can I ever
repay you?

NADEZHDA

Pyotr Ilich, would you now
call me thou
as is the custom
between the closest
of friends?

That is the only fee
I will ever ask of you!

PYOTR ILICH
(scribbling in haste)

Today I went into the mountains
on my own. I love their solitude here,
but I miss Russia so much!
I would come back at once,
if I didn't have to face
those at the Conservatory.

NADEZHDA

People fear what the break-up
of ice will bring.
More typhus, diphtheria
and smallpox, perhaps?

Every day I disinfect my rooms
of the germs,
so you will be safe here
when you return.

> *(CUE IN: PIANO CONCERTO*
> *NO. 1 from 0.33 – 02.12,*[23]
> *BACKGROUNDING until 'to you')*

---

[23] https://www.youtube.com/watch?v=2DmfJu3oNDM

Last night, Rubinstein played your concerto
to a full house. He was equal to the grandeur
of the piece! They brought in laurel wreathes
he dedicated to you.

If only you'd been there!

PYOTR ILICH
(warms to the compliment)

Do I need to repeat
that you are the only one person
I can love with all
my being?

You are as indispensable to me
as air.

I know you will absorb every
note I send!
And yet I still can't address you
by thou.

Why?

NADEZHDA

We must do more
to get you better known abroad,
so you will not feel trapped
at the Conservatory.

(IMAGE of <u>Mikhail GLINKA</u>[24] *on*
CENTRE SCREEN)

You and Glinka are such equal
pearls, yet I strain
to get your music heard anywhere
outside of Russia.

---

[24] https://www.facebook.com/photo/?fbid=113884676691628&set
=a.113883450025084

PYOTR ILICH

Would I ever return to that hated place?

If I resigned,
few students would miss me.
It takes an eternity to hammer things
into their heads, especially the women,
most of whom prefer to be… played
than to play.
   (smiles at his wit)
The weather here has decided to improve
just when I'm about to leave.
The sky is quite clear now,
and only light clouds hover over
the snow-capped mountains
on the other side of the lake.
How annoying!

NADEZHDA

What news from your wife?

PYOTR ILICH

She received my divorce proposal,
and Anatoly will seek an answer
in a week. She'd have to be mad to refuse
10,000 roubles… but mad she is!
   (shivers)
Bad weather chased me all the way
to Kamenka, and the scenery is dreary.
Worst of all

   (IMAGES of GHETTO 1, 2, 3 are projected
   on SCREENS from left to right)[25]

is the Yiddish settlement that fouls the air.

[25] https://acrobat.adobe.com/id/urn:aaid:sc:AP:0a54e965-7102-4c6c-8ca5-d01183b895d6

NADEZHDA

You must go to my house at Brailov then, my dear.
There are charming walks in the forest,
with velvet meadows below, the river
flowing past, and nightingales overhead.

I can't leave Moscow this instant,
but you'll inhale the poetry there
for me, won't you?

Marcel will see to your every wish,
and you can ride horses,
go hunting with the dogs
or simply rest indoors.

You'll have your choice
of grand pianos and sheet music,
though I do recommend you try
the Erard upright in my rooms.

Do have a look at the marble figure
of the sleeping boy when you're there.
I love it, though it reminds me of the son
I lost four years ago.

PYOTR ILICH

That certain personage has proven
to be madder than even I could have imagined!

She told my sister that we are destined
to be reconciled one day
because I really must love her.
Ha! This what I get for not
confronting her in person!
So, last night I wrote to tell her
she has two weeks to sign,
or the lump sum I've offered

will go back to its source.
Meaning you.

> *(CUE IN: SOUVENIR D'UN LIEU*
> *CHER, 0.00-0.45[26], FADING OUT ON*
> *'you anything!')*

Well, I've decided to go to Brailov, after all.
I cannot refuse you anything!

NADEZHDA

How pleasant it is to imagine you
playing my favourite piano, opening
my little bookcases, resting
on a secluded bench in the shade,
thinking God, how good it is here!

> *(PROJECT BRAILOV MONASTERY*
> *on CENTRE SCREEN)[27]*

You must walk to Mariengai Wood
where you'll find an ancient Catholic monastery.
There's a grave of two brothers there
that reminds me of your plan for Onegin
because they were rivals in love.

Does the nightingale sing outside
your window?
Last night, I dreamt
that it was.

PYOTR ILICH

I dreamt of fat red mushrooms last night.
Living close to the forest
makes you become childlike again.

---

[26] https://www.youtube.com/watch?v=F73_CQq9NKQ
[27] https://acrobat.adobe.com/id/urn:aaid:sc:AP:0a54e965-7102-4c6c-8ca5-d01183b895d6

For an hour I watched a snail
being pursued by ants
after it had wandered into their nest.
They reduced it to exhaustion,
Then to a parenthesis.

How that reminds me of life
back in Moscow!
(pauses)
Poor Anatoly is overworked
and in love.
I don't know what is worse for him.
Happily, that certain personage has agreed
to accept the lump sum,
but she has absolutely no idea
what she will have to assert
to have the marriage dissolved
without a scandal.

So, I must cut short my time here in Brailov
and spend the summer in Moscow
to make sure she knows how to behave.

You have no idea how corrupt
the system is there. At every step
the officials, clerks and clerics
must be bribed,
and they don't hesitate to tell you
exactly how much they want!

> *(CUE IN: VIOLIN CONCERTO IN*
> *D MAJOR from 0.04-0.51,[28] FADING*
> *OUT as NADEZHDA begins to speak)*

NADEZHDA

How sad that I missed you in Brailov

---

[28] https://www.youtube.com/watch?v=VMov701K_7A

by only a few days! I consoled myself
with your violin concerto.

> *(CUE IN: VIOLIN CONCERTO*
> *IN D MAJOR from 1.50 to 2.25 as*
> *BACKGROUND)*

It's one of those special pieces
that stays with you, increasing
your pleasure each time you play it.

Yesterday, I went around to every place
you visited while you were here. I felt you
so strongly there I could have reached out
and touched you.

Only in my mind, of course!

PYOTR ILICH

I'm in Kamenka seeing my sister,
who has been in great pain
on account of her bad liver.

This is her worst attack ever,
and the family fears for her.

My wife made it all the worse
by saying she and Anatoly had turned me
against her. Now she insists
that I must come and collapse
at her feet to apologise.

It's such an incredible sea
of nonsense!

NADEZHDA

Yes, *Romeo and Juliet* would make a wonderful opera
in your hands! We will never have enough of that tale,
and the pain that comes when pure love

is poisoned by a hate-inscribed
society.

PYOTR ILICH
*(pours himself more wine and quickly
drains the glass)*
Things have gone from bad to worse here.

My sister's children are falling ill now,
one by one. Young Vera has an abscess in her ear
and Anatoly an inflamed eye.

For some reason I am in perfect health,
if you discount my insomnia and my sudden urges
to bolt away—from everything.

(pours himself another glass)

Luckily, I'm fortified with enough
willpower to hang on—for the family's sake.

NADEZHDA
With this letter, I am leaving you two sums:
the usual one, and 2,500 roubles extra
for a *certain personage*, in hope
that she will finally come to her senses.

I hope you are not drinking too much wine!

(PYOTR ILICH splutters in mid-gulp)

I have reason to join you in depression.
My poor Sasha has lost a second child.
The boy was born strong and healthy,
but he died for no apparent reason
two days later.

So, I have gone to Geneva to be with her.
The poor girl is almost insane with grief,

and she will not be comforted even by her mother.

But, Pyotr Ilich, I know the reason
for your sleeplessness.
You are *overworked*.
I have known so many lives lost
from insufficient rest
that I fear for you.

PYOTR ILICH
My heartfelt condolences to your Sasha.

I know how close you are to her,
and I can only imagine the pain she feels
at her loss.

I am off to report for duty at the Conservatory,
but hopeful that, with your generous support,
I may soon be free from that bondage at least,
not to mention a *certain personage*.

NADEZHDA
Will you join me afterwards in Brailov
to celebrate your new life?

Like you, I prefer my solitude,
but as you know there is a surplus
of space here.

PYOTR ILICH
I've nearly finished Onegin now
and cannot wait to show it to you.

I played it through for a group at a soiree
here last night, and they seemed to enjoy it.

Excuse me for saying this, but I enjoyed it
at least as much as they did, and there were times
I could hardly sing for the lump in my throat.

Yet I doubt that it will work on a big stage.
We have no singers up to it,
and I won't have it done poorly
for the sake of a few roubles.

Perhaps I will come to Brailov, my dear.
How else can my feelings on Onegin be verified
except by you?

NADEZHDA

From what you've said, Anatoly should marry
the young girl who has fallen in love with him.

It's better for two people to be happy
and one temporarily unhappy than for two
to be unhappy all the time while one suffers
from unrequited love.
     (pauses)
A *certain personage* excepted, of course.

PYOTR ILICH

If you only knew how much
I crave—need—that freedom
and how close to perfection
I could bring my work if I had it!

Even now, at the very prospect,
my mind is awash with invention.

I know you want me to rest more in my last few days
at Brailov, but I have no power to fight my nature
when it begins to burn with the impatient flame
of inspiration.

Forgive me!

NADEZHDA

I didn't know what to expect here in Paris.

(CUE IN: THE TEMPEST (0.10-
03.10)[29] as BACKGROUND to
NADEZHDA's dialogue, FADE OUT
on 'with our symphony')

At the concert, they had paired up your *Tempest*
with Anton Rubinstein's *Ivan Grozny*.
The audience was a bit stupid at pieces
they'd never heard before, but I forgot them
as soon as the first notes sounded.

All I could think of was my love for its unseen
creator, and I was ready to hand over my soul to you.

You are so kind to dedicate your new suite to me.
Handle it just as you did with our symphony!

PYOTR ILICH

The newspapers wrote about me even before I got back
to Moscow. They really have it in for the Conservatory,
and Rubinstein in particular,
but I do not escape their tar, either.

I could bear it if they kept to my artistic side,
but, no, they have to probe my private life,
probing for fleshy secrets.

And then, when I was travelling by carriage
from Kiev to Kursk I had to listen to gossip
about my marriage—as well as my madness.
I wanted to jump into the nearest ditch,
never to be seen again.

If it is madness to welcome
the thought of death at times like that,
then I am certainly mad.

---

[29] https://www.youtube.com/watch?v=2ueRfUDIY1A

It is only missing you
that keeps me locked on to the pursuit
of perfection.

NADEZHDA

Thank goodness your time in the wilderness
has passed, Pyotr Ilich.

Europe is ready for you at last!

PYOTR ILICH

But am I—
will I ever be—
ready for Europe?

I've only been back in Moscow for a week,
but already I feel shackled by my slot
at the Conservatory.

If only I could stand down,
quietly, never to return.

I could live
at my sister's in the summer,
at Brailov in the spring and autumn.

Would you hate me if I became even more
dependent on your goodwill?

NADEZHDA

I say at once that I'll be extremely glad
if you leave the Conservatory. It's absurd
that you should have to rely on the tyranny
of a man who is twice your inferior.
> *(circulates among the CHAIRS in the*
> *orchestra, righting a few of them)*
If only you knew how many times
I'd mapped out your life
so that you could spend some time

in the country in Russia
and the rest abroad
realising your destiny.

So, we are entirely at one
on this. I shall winter in Italy again

> *(PROJECT <u>LAKE COMO IMAGE</u>*
> *LEFT, CENTRE and RIGHT*
> *SCREENS sequentially)*[30]

and would be so pleased if you could come
as near as possible to me
at Lago di Como.

We could live down by the shore of the lake.

Or at opposite sides of it, if you prefer.

PYOTR ILICH

I'll soon be a free man,
though I am just a bit miffed about it.

Rubinstein heard me out with the smile
of someone listening
to a spoilt child.

'The Conservatoire will lose a great deal
of prestige,' he said, meaning that the students
wouldn't suffer at all.

At least a *certain personage* is abiding
by the terms of my allowance to her
by making herself scarce, but now
I am being bombarded by letters from her mother,
professing her daughter's undying love.

---

[30] https://acrobat.adobe.com/id/urn:aaid:sc:AP:fee9ccb6-29f6-4759-b43c-f4ca5fb29677

She's begging me to be her proxy father
if I can no longer be her husband.

And I thought I was mad!

> ### NADEZHDA
> I'm deeply disturbed by your remedy `
> for pain, my dear.
>
> If you love me even a little,
> you must resist taking too much wine,
> and look after your talent,
> for the sake of others.
>
> Please, go to my house
> and stay as long as you like.
> Ivan Vasil'ev will look after
> your every need in my stead.

> ### PYOTR ILICH
> Yesterday, I did as you asked, my dear,
> and spent two hours in your abode.
>
> It is a wonderful house. But most of all
> I liked your private apartments
>
> and the rooms Ivan had readied for me.
>
> Unfortunately, living there indefinitely
> is still impossible.
>
> While at the Conservatory, I must deal
> with people from my own address.
> Can you imagine Rubinstein's glee
> if he found out I'd settled
> in your house?
> > *(pours himself more wine and toasts
> > her)*
>
> But I do believe wine… in moderation
> does no one harm.

Yet, if I ever feel tempted to excess,
I'll think of you…
> *(balances the glass on his head)*

and make a cancelation
against my inclinations.
> *(catches the glass as it falls and refills it)*

To the fine wines of Italy!

> *(BLACKOUT: SUGGESTED
> INTERMISSION)*

ACT 3

SCENE 1: ANYWHERE BUT MOSCOW

SETTING: As before, with their DESKS and CHAIRS, but with the orchestra CHAIRS, MUSIC STANDS and INSTRUMENTS restored to a semblance of order, the PIANO still in line with the PODIUM at STAGE REAR.

AT RISE: SOFT SIDELIGHTS. CUE IN EUGENE ONEGIN 1[31] from 01:15 to 03:17. PYOTR ILICH paces alone, STAGE FRONT, finally climbing the PODIUM into a BLUE OVERHEAD SPOTLIGHT.

PYOTR ILICH
(to the audience)
I could see it coming in a rush
—my new life.

I'd withdrawn from the Conservatory,
Onegin was ready to burst onto the stage,
concert halls all over Europe were lining up
to play my music, not as a *filler* this time,
but as prime billing.

Even a *certain personage* had stuffed soft rags
in her mouth for the moment, at least.

And Nadezhda Filaretovna waited for me
in Italy like a warm slipper
by the fire.
> *(pauses, then steps off the PODIUM to*
> *begin pacing again)*

---
[31] https://www.youtube.com/watch?v=l_pYA5N4T4k

Why did I hesitate
to embrace my almost perfect match?

She wasn't flawless,
but then how could she have been
any more perfect than I deserve?

Like me, she had a secret
she didn't dare to reveal.

NADEZHDA
(ENTERS, followed by a SOFT GOLD SPOTLIGHT, moving
between the orchestra CHAIRS, tidying them even more)
If only you could come to Florence, my love,
before going on to Clarens.

I leave for Vienna in six weeks

and would so much like to be
near you until then.

I'd set you up in an apartment in Florence

> *(PROJECT FLORENCE IMAGES:*
> FLORENCE APARTMENT *on LEFT*
> *SCREEN; APARTMENT WITH PIANO*
> *ROOM, CENTRE;* FLORENCE AT
> NIGHT *on RIGHT SCREEN)*[32]

where you could get on uninterrupted
with your music.

Thank you for the printed score of Eugene Onegin,
which I received yesterday.

What a ravishing work,
especially the scenes with Ta'iana's letter
and the duel. You made my heart beat faster

[32] https://acrobat.adobe.com/id/urn:aaid:sc:AP:fee9ccb6-29f6-4759-b43c-f4ca5fb29677

and my thoughts soar!

PYOTR ILICH
(to the audience)

Could she *ever* find fault with my music!

Or was this just telling me what
I wanted to hear?

Perhaps if I seem a bit too eager…

You want me to drop everything
to be with you in Florence.
How can I refuse you anything?

Though I am still worried about Tolia.
He has excellent health and a pretty girl
to love him, yet he's deeply depressed
and perpetually irritated.

If he were merely anti-social like me
I'd understand it,
but *everyone* likes him
he loves socialising
and yet…

NADEZHDA
(taken aback)

Your kindness touches me deeply,
but there must be many others
who need your attention more than I.

So, please refuse to come
if you have even the slightest
disinclination.

PYOTR ILICH

Nonsense.

For once, I won't obey you.
I will leave for Florence in a week.
        (to the audience)
We'll see what we shall see
of that.

By the way, my dear, the score of *Onegin*
was supposed to come to me, not to you.
But it had 'Nad. Fil. v. M'
on it, so my servant Alexis sent it to you.

Never mind.
Just have it waiting for me
in Florence, and all will be well.

        (CUE IN: EUGENE ONEGIN,[33] from
        53:28 to 55.07)

NADEZHDA

How glad I am
that you have arrived.

To feel you near me,
to know the rooms you are in,
to admire the same
views as you, to feel the same
temperature as you,
is such bliss that words
can't express!

PYOTR ILICH
        (to the audience)
I am drenched in a sweat of nerves
as I read this—I can almost feel her pen
strokes from the next room!

---

[33] https://www.youtube.com/watch?v=l_pYA5N4T4k

Dearest Nadezhda Filaretovna,
I'd follow you to the remotest corner
of the world, if that were your wish.

*(PROJECT ARNO RIVER AT NIGHT on
CENTRE SCREEN)*[34]

On my first day, I walked as you recommended
from our suite down to the Arno.
The evening was quiet
except for the sound of the swirling water
in the distance.

But today the weather has broken.

I'm afraid I've brought you rain.

NADEZHDA
(to the audience)

Our suite!
My dearest… friend. I must confess
that yesterday evening, we drove past
your door. There were candles lit
in the dining room, so I thought
you must be occupied by dinner.

I rearranged things, so that your bedroom
is on the sunny side.

Do you find my piano
to your liking?

PYOTR ILICH
(to the audience)

There is such a thing as too much
peace and luxury. Her closeness does
unsettle me.

---

[34] https://acrobat.adobe.com/id/urn:aaid:sc:AP:0a54e965-7102-4c6c-8ca5-d01183b895d6

At least in Moscow, I could be distracted
by strangers quickly forgotten.
> *(backs away)*
She often gazes in on her walks.
We are bound to meet one day.

Today, she even sent me a ticket
to the theatre for Saturday night…

NADEZHDA

A *solo* one, I assure you.

I'm sure you'll enjoy the Shakespeare.

PYOTR ILICH

And she's invited me to see the inside
of her villa—while she's away, of course.

NADEZHDA

Not a soul
will be there—I swear!

PYOTR ILICH

Hmm.

NADEZHDA

Some other time, then.

But I'm glad you are thinking about
composing another opera.
> *(mimes gazing through a window)*
In half an hour or so,
we'll be walking past your house.

PYOTR ILICH

Suddenly, I feel totally consumed!
> *(regains control, clearing his throat)*
I must lend you the delightful satire
I am reading about that detestable Jew, Disraeli.

It's a pity that things are going
so well for his lot
in Afghanistan.

Ah, yes, and I'm also enclosing a telegram
prattling on about the success of our symphony.

I'm terribly pleased!

Modest said the applause after the first movement
was as if the piece had been a Beethoven,
and after the Scherzo there were *fortissimo*
shouts, stomping feet and demands for an encore.
Then, even before the finale had been heard,
the audience went mad again!

NADEZHDA

I knew it would be just a matter of time
for our symphony.

PYOTR ILICH

When I wrote it, I hardly knew you,
but now I see that you understand better
than anyone what this offspring of ours
means to the demanding world…
            (turns to the audience)
But now my work on the *new* suite
has ground to a halt.

It's *she*.

She wants to *see* me —
and more.

In her letters, she's kept
a tactful distance.
Until now.

NADEZHDA

My first waking thoughts are of you.

And all through the day your presence
seems to punctuate the very air.

How happy I am to have gotten to know you.

In just two hours' time
I shall be walking past your sanctuary.
What a pleasure!

PYOTR ILICH
(clutches at his throat)
Is she closing in for the kill?
(SCRIBBLES hastily)
The charm and poetry of our friendship
overflows with your being so near to me,
while at the same time
I do not know you at all
in that… tactile sense of the word.
(tightens his grip)
Some air.
I need some air!

> *(He begins darting between the*
> *ORCHESTRA CHAIRS, while she*
> *walks wistfully to STAGE CENTRE,*
> *just missing colliding with him. On*
> *the verge of intersection, they freeze*
> *briefly.)*

Nadezhda Filaretovna!

NADEZHDA

Pyotr Ilich!

(Seemingly cornered, they edge this way and that, avoiding touch, trying to get the best angle at which to view the other. They are curious, excited, apprehensive. They speak at once to the audience, with furtive glances back at each other.)

PYOTR ILICH

Sorry, I left a bit early after dinner.
(breathless)
Just a bit early.

NADEZHDA

Sorry, I returned a bit late for dinner.
(breathless)
Only a few minutes.

PYOTR ILICH
(apologetic)
You first.

NADEZHDA

No, you.

PYOTR ILICH
(desperate)
You are quite… beautiful!

NADEZHDA

Am I?

Not hopelessly your senior?

PYOTR ILICH

F-forgive me!

(She seems to encourage something more from him, but he looks confused,

*finally tipping an imaginary HAT
then backing off to STAGE REAR,
glancing off a few ORCHESTRA
CHAIRS in his haste, ducking behind
the PIANO. Her eyes follow him, she
sighs, straightening the CHAIRS, then
reluctantly exits. PYOTR ILICH raises
his hand as if to say something, but
nothing comes out. He gets down on
his hands and knees.)*

PYOTR ILICH
*(extending a hand to the audience from
the shelter of the PIANO)*
Afterwards, I wandered through the forest
in a daze.

I told myself that I was fossicking
for mushrooms.
*(struggles to his feet, hitting his head
on the PIANO BENCH, almost losing
his balance, but working his way to
STAGE FRONT)*
Her cheeks were flushed.
Yes, definitely flushed.

And so, our dream must, *must be*
shattered. Dissolved.
I should have known better
than to dance with fire!

*(NADEZHDA reappears, preens
herself in front of an imaginary
MIRROR then turns away.)*

NADEZHDA
He lied

for my sake:
I *am* much too old
for him.

I'll be dead long before him,
and he'll forget me
in a day,
or two at most.
> *(breaks into tears)*
Oh, have I ruined everything?!

PYOTR ILICH
(cupping his hands)
I came upon the fattest mushrooms
that evening—what did that mean?

And when I came back to the house for tea,
there was yet another letter from her.

Alexis says her man came with it
on horseback.
> *(reacts with horror and disbelief as he
> holds up the imaginary LETTER)*

NADEZHDA
*(approaches to read over his shoulder,
miming her words)*
Nikolai Rubinstein has passed, my love.

The reports are so dreadful. It seems
he was on holiday and just… dropped dead
of a ruptured heart, in the street.

They packed his body into a leadened coffin
and shipped it back to Moscow in a luggage van.

Shame!
He was buried yesterday

in the cold rain and mud
with hardly more mourners
than for Mozart.

PYOTR ILICH
(dazed)
He did deserve better than that.

NADEZHDA
But don't you see:
I WISHED HIM DEAD!!

PYOTR ILICH
(clutches the imaginary LETTER,
fingers shaking)
But… why?

NADEZHDA
He was furious about your resignation.

He accused me of putting you up to it.
And of luring you into… an affair.

He threatened to go to the papers
if I didn't promise
to drag you back at once.

PYOTR ILICH
(with the LETTER at arm's length)
No, I *was* a wretched teacher.

Too preoccupied.
Slave to selfishness.

He knew that.

He seemed resolved to replace me
with Taneev.
(thinks about it)

He was so… polite when I told him
of my plan to resign!

                    NADEZHDA

He was a horrible, horrible man.
He would have ruined you for… this.
And us.

                    PYOTR ILICH

Well, my conscience is clean.

We have never… done anything!

                    NADEZHDA
                    (to the audience)

No.

On that, we are one.

                    PYOTR ILICH

But now you must stay away from me.
Far away.

                    *(NADEZHDA turns the other cheek as
                    though he's just slapped her, sets her
                    jaw firmly, exits.)*

What else was I to do
in my stumbling way?

If I had known it would come to this.
That it would play straight into the hands
of a *certain personage*. Just as I was on the verge
of being embraced by the musical world,
just as I was about to put all worries
about material things into the past.

                    NADEZHDA
                    (OFF STAGE)

Again, and again:
I'm sorry.

Sorry.

PYOTR ILICH
(to the audience)
I had to put her behind me.
No choice.

I'd ride the crest of Onegin and Joan of Ark
to prosperity and not have to depend on anyone.

So, I packed my bags again for Russia
where I bought a comfortable house in Maidanovo,
which I furnished with no more
than my absolute necessities.

I've retained Alexis to look after my daily needs
and my nephew Vladmir for… conversation.

NADEZHDA
(reappears, hesitantly)
You do not answer my letters.

I do completely understand.
But please take the funds.

Can I not still look after you.
As we were?

PYOTR ILICH
I didn't write back for months.
And thankfully the whispers seemed to die down.
Not a whiff of scandal remained.

Perhaps it *had* been my fault.

Perhaps I had put the wrong wishes
in her mind.

(clears his throat)
But then *Onegin* didn't bring in quite as much
as I'd expected.

So, I began to write back again.

More carefully than before.

PYOTR ILICH

NADEZHDA
(cynically)
Carefully?

PYOTR ILICH
And not as often…

NADEZHDA
Certainly not as often!

> *(She approaches him cautiously,*
> *circling, moving in. He does not react.*
> *She comes up behind him and firmly*
> *embraces him — still no reaction.*
> *Their actions follow what he's about to*
> *say, though there is no passion on his*
> *part.)*

PYOTR ILICH
(sighs)
Sometimes I *am* overcome by an insane
craving for the caress
of a woman's touch.
(tortured)
In my dreams I see a beautiful woman
in whose lap I could lay my head.
Whose fingertips I would gladly compense
with a sincere kiss…
(shakes himself out of it and

backs away)
My niece Tatiana died last night at a masked ball
in Petersburg.

(CUE IN: LES CAPRICES D'OXANE
(1.42-2.18)[35]

Just as I had to conduct
my *Les Caprices d'Oxane* in Moscow
(conflicted)
but the concert went well. I can conduct, after all!

(Each addresses the audience in turn
to argue their case.)

NADEZHDA
He was coming back to me—I was sure of it.

PYOTR ILICH
(embarrassed)
I was living in her house again.
(pauses)
I saw no reason to deprive myself
of the greatest... friendship I'd ever had.

NADEZHDA
(almost girl-like)
We teased on like that...

PYOTR ILICH
...for years.
A decade, more or less.

It seemed we'd survived that rough patch
and redefined our fences.

NADEZHDA
But he never got his divorce.

[35] https://www.youtube.com/watch?v=zqb1le8E2ak

PYOTR ILICH

It was too hard in the end.
She was threatening—

NADEZHDA

Safer, that way.

For him.

PYOTR ILICH

Boundaries, my dear,
limits.

NADEZHDA

Then, *suddenly*…

PYOTR ILICH
(harshly)
Yes, suddenly… Nothing.

NADEZHDA
(protests)
I tried to explain!

PYOTR ILICH

About *nada*.

NADEZHDA

The emperor had awarded you a lifetime annuity
of 3,000 roubles, and you were playing to sell-outs
in Leipzig and Prague.

All richly deserved, and long past due,
but you didn't need me anymore!

PYOTR ILICH

That was not the point.
It was never about the money!

NADEZHDA

It *was*. But somewhere along the way…

When did we—you—change?

PYOTR ILICH
(intones)
Can you recognise in this Russian musician,
touring all over Europe, the man who,
a few years ago, fled,
tail between his legs,
from life and society?

NADEZHDA

You see?

PYOTR ILICH

So, you wrote to me again and again—

NADEZHDA
(finishes for him)
About nothing.

I was financially ruined.
I wouldn't have been able
to support you.

PYOTR ILICH

I would have supported you
if you'd given me half the chance.

Then at least we could have been square.
(clenches his fists)
But the truth was, you weren't ruined.

NADEZHDA

I was!

PYOTR ILICH

Scant measures later you were rich again.

NADEZHDA

(quickly)

There was no need for you to repay me.

It was I who was in your debt, all along.

PYOTR ILICH

After all those years. WHY?

NADEZHDA

(in agony)

All right.

The truth, then.

Remember my daughter Sasha.

The one who had the stillborn babes?

PYOTR ILICH

Of course. I sent her flowers.

NADEZHDA

You never told me that!

PYOTR ILICH

I signed it 'from a friend of the family'.

NADEZHDA

She told me…

(breaks off)

something so horrible

that I had no choice with you.

PYOTR ILICH

I… don't understand!

NADEZHDA

(tenderly)

Do you remember my little Milochka
The one who mistook you
for the King of Bavaria?

PYOTR ILICH

The sweet child I saw at the concert?

NADEZHDA

Well, I had her out of wedlock.

One night's mistake... with a stranger.

PYOTR ILICH
(initially at a loss)

And you didn't confess to your husband?

NADEZHDA

I… couldn't.

I was so ashamed.

Finally, I had to tell someone.

PYOTR ILICH

Sasha?

NADEZHDA
(nods)

I made her promise not to tell her father.
But she did, and it brought on his heart attack.

She kept the secret festering inside
for all those years!

PYOTR ILICH
(it dawns on him)

She blamed you.

NADEZHDA

For his death.

And now her lost babies.

PYOTR ILICH
But why tell you now — after all these years?

NADEZHDA
It was you who had abandoned me,
and I had no one to talk to.

When I told her of our… friendship,
she remembered the notes you sent to Milochka
and jumped to the wrong conclusions.

PYOTR ILICH
But that was years before we met!

NADEZHDA
I told her that.

But then she seized on the many pieces of music
you dedicated to me, the many rumours she'd heard
over the years, and, yes,
even the flowers you sent—

PYOTR ILICH
I would have spoken to her.

I would have *told* her—

NADEZHDA
She made me swear, for her silence,
that I would break it off with you.
(sees his hurt)
Pyotr Ilich, I hadn't heard from you for months,
and before that for weeks.

You were realising your destiny,
so it seemed a small cost to say
what already was implied.

*(They stand staring at each other. CUE
IN: ONEGIN[36] from 1.15.30–1.16.39[37]
as BACKGROUND.)*

PYOTR ILICH

I tried to tell you.

Didn't you know?

If there ever could have been
a woman for me
it would have been you.

NADEZHDA

I heard it, in your letters,
and your music.

How many times I wished
that I could have found the right aria
to answer you.

But words on their own are too dangerous,
too… close to the heart.

*(CUE IN: ONEGIN from 1.18.15-
1:19.29,[38] as BACKGROUND, slowly
intensifying. During the music/dance,
he takes a step toward her, and they
embrace, stiffly on his part at first but
then he warms up to it.)*

PYOTR ILICH

The music wasn't enough after all.

It was my fault.

---

[36] https://www.youtube.com/watch?v=l_pYA5N4T4k
[37] https://www.youtube.com/watch?v=l_pYA5N4T4k
[38] https://www.youtube.com/watch?v=l_pYA5N4T4k

NADEZHDA
(kisses her finger and puts it to his lips)

No, mine.

I knew who you were,
but I could not stop myself.

I had to have all of you
Or nothing.

PYOTR ILICH

I cursed you on my deathbed, you know.

They were the only words I got out.

NADEZHDA

And I heard every word,
from the other side of never!

(They hold each other at arm's length and then laugh. They walk slowly toward EXIT STAGE LEFT, arm in arm.)

PYOTR ILICH

It would make a grand opera, don't you think
Our story?

NADEZHDA

A tone poem, at best.

Besides, who would finance it?
You were always hopeless
with sums!

(They EXIT. CUE IN: <u>ONEGIN</u> from 2:25.26-2.26.40 to FADE OUT)[39]

—ENDS—

---

[39] https://www.youtube.com/watch?v=l_pYA5N4T4k

Endnotes

[1] https://en.tchaikovsky-research.net/pages/Nadezhda_von_Meck
[2] https://www.abc.net.au/classic/read-and-watch/music-reads/classically-curious-tchaikovsky-von-meck/11288844